MY AWESOME Glam Ma and ME

Bernice Lowe Flowers, Author   Rakiyah Lowe Kelly, Co-Author

To order additional copies of this book, contact:
Xlibris
844-714-8691
www.Xlibris.com
Orders@Xlibris.com

ISBN: Softcover   978-1-6641-6691-2
        Hardcover   978-1-6641-6692-9
        EBook   978-1-6641-6693-6

Library of Congress Control Number: 2021907057

Print information available on the last page

Rev. date: 06/24/2021

MY AWESOME
Glam Ma
and ME

Bernice Lowe Flowers

Author

Rakiyah Lowe Kelly

Co-Author

Illustrated by: Tammy Turner

TODAY
some grandmothers see

themselves as

younger, savvy,

and glamorous

than their grandmothers

when they were

little girls,

so they now consider

themselves

GLAM MAS

NOWADAYS, grandmothers are much more active, healthier, tolerant in their attitude and expectations, don't get bent out of shape easily by every day nuisances and disappointments, and seem to be more realistic at seeing the world as it is instead of how they would prefer it to be.

2

In this book,

I share some special moments spent

with my Glam Ma.

I call my grandmother Glam Ma

because she is

glamorous, smart, lively, fun, amazing,

and has her own personal style.

This book is dedicated to girls who share a special
bond with their Glam Mas

My name is Sunny and I am a cheerful

and bubbly little girl.

My parents named me Sunny

because

I was born on a bright summer's day.

When a baby girl is born,

there's a special bond

between the baby and grandmother.

As the baby girl grows older,

the relationship she cultivates with her

grandmother becomes stronger,

and she learns to appreciate

the wisdom, advice, support and fun

shared between them

that no one can shatter easily.

Welcome Little One,

I am so excited

to meet you.

You are a new

addition to our

wonderful family

and

we love you

dearly!

Glam Ma plays, sings,

and cuddles with me.

Her voice is calming

and puts me to sleep...

8

On sunny days, Glam Ma and Mommy take me to the park where I can enjoy the fresh air and sunshine that are necessary and good for my health.

9

We see squirrels
and hear birds chirping little songs

10

It's yummy time!

Glam Ma feeds me

fresh vegetables and fruits everyday

especially, carrots and bananas.

Eating nutritious food makes me

healthy, strong, and prevents me

from getting sick.

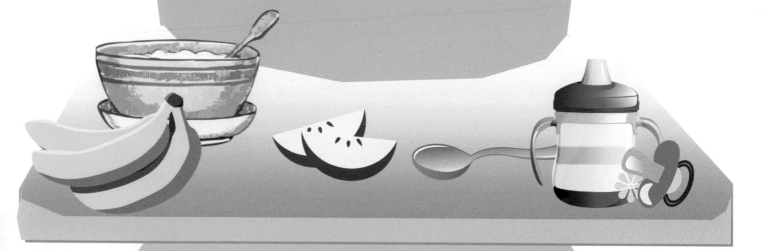

Glam Ma gives me a warm

bubble bath before putting me to bed!

I like to play in the warm soapy water...

So refreshing and relaxing!

When Mommy is busy,

Glam Ma takes and picks

me up from school.

15

I enjoy the short walk home,

listening to the birds and

watching people walk their pets.

16

Glam Ma shares her love of gardening with me.

She plants her favorite vegetables,

and I help her water the soil

to keep the plants healthy.

Glam Ma teaches me how to make

cakes and cookies.

Can't wait to sample the ingredients

she dumps into the mixing bowl.

Get moving with Glam Ma!

21

Exercising and having fun is a great way

for us to stay active and healthy.

Glam Ma and I go to the library regularly...

a special place with rules

where everyone has to be very quiet.

Sometimes,

I read books or play games on the computer.

READING
is FUN!

Enjoying a meal at a restaurant with Glam Ma...

Pizza and ice cream

are my favorite items on the menu!

27

Traveling with Glam Ma

allows me to experience the world,

learn about other people,

and gives us a

chance to sample delicious foods.

Going to Church...

a special experience I share with my Glam Ma.

We listen to the preacher,

say prayers,

and sing hymns.

I love and appreciate my Glam Ma so much!
I admire her emotional strength, composure,
patience, kindness, willingness to listen,
and her unconditional love.
Because my Glam Ma
is such a special person
and for all the wonderful
things she does for me,

31

I give her cards, flowers, kisses,

and heartwarming hugs.

Glam Ma you are precious!

About the Author

Bernice Lowe Flowers is a voice for change. She is a Journalist and Change Agent with a calming, nurturing, and welcoming presence that makes people feel comfortable and at ease about themselves. She collaborates with individuals and organizations that support people in discovering themselves, and uses creativity, tangible tools, and strategic practices to support individuals in addressing their fears and developing a place where everyone has an equal voice.

Printed in the United States
by Baker & Taylor Publisher Services